THE VANISHING VILLAGE

Sarah Dixon

Illustrated by Brenda Haw

Designed by Adrienne Kern

Edited by Karen Dolby

Series Editor: Gaby Waters

Additional designs by Kim Blundell and Stephen Wright

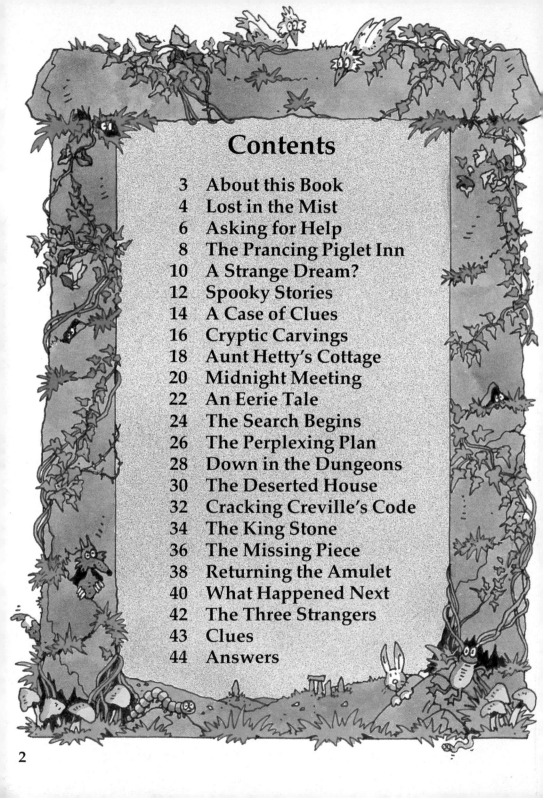

Contents

About this Book

The Vanishing Village is a spooky story about a strange village that mysteriously appears at midnight and vanishes without trace by dawn.

Throughout the book, there are lots of ghostly puzzles and perplexing problems which you must solve in order to understand the next part of the story.

Look at the pictures carefully and watch out for vital clues. Sometimes you will need to flick back through the book to help you find an answer. There are extra clues on page 43 and you can check the answers on pages 44 to 48.

Just turn the page to begin the adventure . . .

Aunt Hetty

Ben

Jay

Jay and Ben set off to explore the moors around the village of Little Snoozing, where they are staying with Aunt Hetty. She has been telling them ghostly tales about the ruined castles, deserted manor houses and ancient standing stones on the moors.

Lost in the Mist

Jay and Ben stumbled through the rough grass, looking for the path back to Little Snoozing. It was dark and a swirling, purple mist surrounded them. They were cold and lost.

Ben spotted the blurred outlines of stones on top of a hill, just visible through the mist ahead. He dug into his rucksack for his map. There was a dull ripping sound and it fell to pieces in his hands.

"We'll never find our way back now," Jay groaned.

SPLASH! She found herself skidding into a pool of icy water. She squelched back to dry land and yanked off her soggy boots. As she tipped out the water, a strange piece of metal fell out of her left boot.

Suddenly a bell tolled in the distance. One, two, three . . . twelve strokes. Was it really midnight? Jay glanced at her watch but it had stopped. At least the mist was beginning to clear. She saw lights glowing in the valley below. Soon she could even make out the outlines of houses in a village.

**Look at Ben's map.
Can you find the village on it?**

5

Asking for Help

It was very confusing. The village was in Mourne Valley, but nothing was marked on Ben's map. Feeling cold and tired, they decided to go down to the mysterious village and ask for help.

As they walked along the cobbled streets, a tingling sensation crept down their necks. Jay shivered. There was no one around except for a girl and a pig. When Ben asked her how to get to Little Snoozing, she looked puzzled.

"Ask Harold," she said. "He'll help you. He's the innkeeper at The Prancing Piglet. I'd take you there myself, but I'm in a hurry. You can see the inn from here. It's the half-timbered building with the tiled roof, two chimneys and two attic windows."

Jay and Ben stared at the jumble of roof-tops ahead. Which one was the inn?

Can you find the inn?

The Prancing Piglet Inn

They clattered down the narrow streets towards the inn. Ben tugged a thick rope next to the door and a bell clanged loudly. Immediately, the door opened and a man peered out.

"Come in," he said, smiling. "I'm Harold, the innkeeper."

They followed Harold into a warm, cheerful room with a roaring log fire.

8

"We're trying to get back to Little Snoozing," Jay explained. "Aunt Hetty will be worried. Can you help us?"

"It's very late and too dark to set off now," Harold said. "You can stay here. I'll make sure your aunt gets a message."

Just then, a boy the same age as Jay and Ben walked in and gave them a friendly grin.

"Could you find these two a room, Thomas?" asked Harold.

Jay was about to protest, but before she could say a word, she began to feel strangely at home in the inn. She was so warm and comfortable in the large wooden armchair by the fire. It would be a long, tiring journey back in the darkness and mist . . . Of course they should stay! She yawned sleepily.

A Strange Dream?

Ben was tucking into a hearty breakfast at The Prancing Piglet and was just about to ask Harold if he could phone Aunt Hetty, when . . . OUCH! He woke up with a jolt. A sharp stone dug into his side. The sun dazzled his eyes. He was outside, back on Bleak Moor. Feeling confused, he shook Jay awake.

"What's happening?" she mumbled, rubbing her eyes. "What are we doing here? Where's Harold and Thomas and the village inn?"

They turned to look down into the valley, but the roof-tops and cobbled streets had vanished. All they could see were trees and more trees. Could they really have imagined it all?

How weird! It seemed so real – the village, the girl with the pig, the inn, Harold's homemade soup, the comfortable bed . . .

As they tramped through the heather towards Little Snoozing, Jay had a vivid flashback. She was lying in her bed at the inn, half-asleep. In front of her stood a shadowy figure who was trying to tell her something.

"But that sounds just like my dream," Ben gasped, when Jay described what she remembered.

They stared at one another in disbelief. They had both had the same dream – identical, except the figure had said different things. In their dreams, the words had seemed strange and jumbled, but as Jay and Ben repeated them, they realized the words made an eerie message.

What is the message?

We your help. Curse taken its. Our has vanished are in eternal. You release us. Back us and explain. But remember must something from with.

Need. The ancient has terrible revenge. Village and we trapped limbo. Only can. Please come to I will everything. That you bring this village you.

Spooky Stories

Back in Little Snoozing, Jay spotted Aunt Hetty disappearing into the Greasy Spoon Cafe.

"Aunt Hetty!" Jay cried, running into the cafe.

"I got your message," Aunt Hetty smiled.

So a message HAD been sent... But who had sent it? Harold? But that meant their night in the village was real. But if the village was real, why had it vanished by the morning?

"How strange," Jay muttered.

"What is?" asked Aunt Hetty.

"Everything," said Ben. "The message and the village and Mourne Valley..."

"Oh, Mourne Valley's strange all right," piped up an old man.

And this started everyone off. There seemed to be hundreds of mysteries and eerie tales about Mourne Valley. Ben looked around, then gasped in amazement. Perhaps some of the tales were true!

What has Ben realized?

There is an old tale about a mysterious village in Mourne Valley that vanished into thin air hundreds of years ago. Of course, no one really believes it.

Little Snoozing ANNUAL JUMBLE SALE 30th April 9–4 in aid of Insomniacs Anonymous

Some say you can hear a ghostly bell in the valley.

Legend says that the ghostly village only appears on the last three nights of the fourth month when the bell tolls twelve times... It's just a story, though.

Have you heard the one about the peddlar who found a goblet from the phantom village and claimed he walked into the village that very night?

A Case of Clues

Yawn…

They decided to take Aunt Hetty's advice and go to the museum. They slurped down their milkshakes and set off, determined to find out more about the mystery village.

The museum looked dismally dreary inside. There were no costumes, no suits of armour and no model castles.

Jay peered into the dusty glass cases one by one. King Hengist's stamp collection. The last will of D. Wisp. How boring and useless. Then she spotted a small case tucked away in a dingy corner.

"There used to be a REAL village in Mourne Valley," she exclaimed to Ben, minutes later. "I've even found out its name."

Ben looked blank.

"Remember the villages on your map and the picture in the inn?" she said. "They gave me a clue."

What is the name of the village?

Milk Monitor

The Phantom of Gloome Towers

Silas and Titus – the Wayle Twins ag...

This survey covers all villages in Woldshire

Mme Burstiere - Corset Maker to the Gentry. Customers - May 1670

Much Flooding	1
Thunder Magna	2½
Snowe-on-the-Wold	0
Stormy Wether	41
Cloud Magna	-2
Sleet	20
Long Blizzard	49
Wraithe-dtle-Mourne	3
Much Plagued	0
Drislington	5

Alice Creville — aged 4

Owners of Potboilers and Sundry Thrillers May 1672

Sleet.	
Drislington.	10
Long Blizzard.	200
Thunder Magna.	3
Much Flooding.	1½
Little Snoozing.	33
Stormy Wether.	0
Cloud Magna.	6
Snowe-on-the-Wold.	2¾
	5

(This survey covers all villages in Woldshire)

Lucky Wishbone

Shopping List
1 partric pear
2 call
3 f
4

Will's picklefork

Sir Waldo Raleigh's Potato Knife

Ebenezer Wayle aged 6

Identity Card
Name — Groan
Job — Creville's Chef

Family Crests

The Tenant of Wildmoor Hall   Lord Gloome   Lord Howlingale

Sir Gervaise Creville   Will Chill   Abbot of Crumbledown

Identity Card
Name — GRUMBLE
Job — CREVILLE's butler

Lord Gloome and family at rest - 1677

Readers of Witch Magazine April 1668

1 Much Plagued.
1 Long Blizzard.
0 Drislington.
2 Sleet.
1 Wraithe-atte-Mourne.
2 Much Flooding.
1 Drowne-under-Bleak.
0 Stormy Wether.
1 Little Snoozing.
4 Cloud Magna.
0 Snowe-on-the-Wold.
   Thunder Magna.

This List covers all villages in Woldshire.

Hovel and Garden
Subscriptions covering all villages in Woldshire March 1672

Much Flooding _____ 1
Snowe-on-the-Wold ___ 2
Wraithe-atte-Mourne __ 10
Cloud Magna _____ ½
Thunder Magna _____ 6
Long Blizzard _____ 7
Little Snoozing _____ 3
Drislington _____ 4
Stormy Wether _____ 0
Sleet _____ 3
             8

Lady Wayle's Beauty Lotion

Lord Crumhorn alias Red Arrow - highwayman

Alice's Joy Duck

The Headless Ghost of Wildmoor Castle - as seen by Claire Vayant

15

Cryptic Carvings

Ben was amazed. More than three hundred years ago, there had been a village in Mourne Valley, called Wraithe-atte-Mourne. Then suddenly the village had vanished. But how?

As Ben wandered away from the case, he spotted something interesting across the room. He barged past some yawning tourists to take a closer look. It was a sundial from Wraithe-atte-Mourne. Its base was decorated with strange carvings.

"What are they?" Jay asked.

"They're words written in Sombric Script," said the curator, coming up behind them.

She handed them an old book and added, "There's a chapter on Sombric Script in here. It should help you work out what the carvings say".

Ben impatiently flicked through the book. Perhaps the sundial would tell them more about Wraithe.

Can you work out what the carvings say?

16

16ᵗʰ century Sundial from Wraithe-atte-Mourne donated by Dawn Korus

Herbert's wine-making kit

Otto's odds & ends pot

Pots of fun for everyone

...teresting ...ecimen of

Mug pieces found near Little Snoozing by B. Kerr in 1850

The Mug People

The Mugs lived in Mourne Valley thousands of years ago. They were named after their custom of burying their dead with brightly-coloured mugs and ample supplies of coffee and drinking chocolate to keep them awake during their journey to the underworld.

The Mugs are famous for the standing stones on Sombre Hill (sometimes wrongly called a stone circle). The arrangement of the stones appears jumbled, but they are in fact arranged in 14 rows, running north to south. Each row contains between two and seven stones, and there are large gaps between some of them. There are also four single stones which stand alone in the group. The very famous UFO specialist, Don Vannikin, claims these rows are landing markers for ancient extra-terrestrials and are still regularly used as a refuelling point.

The Mugs told many stories and carved them onto disused standing stones in Sombric Script. In 1888 Sir Diggory Fyndes translated their famous saga, Bare Wilf, from Sombric Script, using his Grid Principle. There are no gaps between words in Sombric Script and numbers are written as upright strokes – 1 is one, 11 is two, etc.

A B C D E F G H I J K L M N
O P Q R S T U V W X Y Z

The Sombric Alphabet

17

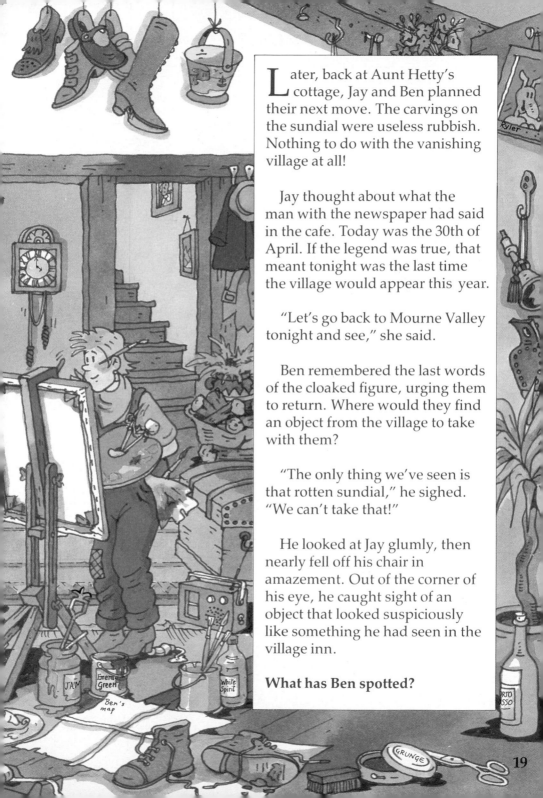

Later, back at Aunt Hetty's cottage, Jay and Ben planned their next move. The carvings on the sundial were useless rubbish. Nothing to do with the vanishing village at all!

Jay thought about what the man with the newspaper had said in the cafe. Today was the 30th of April. If the legend was true, that meant tonight was the last time the village would appear this year.

"Let's go back to Mourne Valley tonight and see," she said.

Ben remembered the last words of the cloaked figure, urging them to return. Where would they find an object from the village to take with them?

"The only thing we've seen is that rotten sundial," he sighed. "We can't take that!"

He looked at Jay glumly, then nearly fell off his chair in amazement. Out of the corner of his eye, he caught sight of an object that looked suspiciously like something he had seen in the village inn.

What has Ben spotted?

19

Midnight Meeting

T hat night, Jay and Ben scrambled through the heather to the pool on the top of Bleak Moor, clutching the silver spoon. In the distance a bell tolled twelve times.

Their hearts pounded as they gazed at Mourne Valley below. Would the village appear again?

"Look!" Ben cried. "Lights... and houses!"

He raced down towards the village with Jay panting behind him. A familiar tingling sensation ran down their necks when they reached the first cottages in the valley.

A maze of winding streets led them past more cottages and a bell tower to a small village square and a river with stepping stones. Jay leapt onto the first stone, then...

20

"Over here!" hissed a voice.

SPLASH! Jay lost her balance and found herself knee-deep in icy water again. A cloaked figure holding a lantern stood in front of her. It was the person they had seen last night.

"Come with me," the figure said. "We must talk."

Ben hesitated. Who was this mysterious hooded character and what did he want?

Suddenly, Ben caught sight of the figure's face, lit for an instant by the glow from the lantern. He grinned. So that's who it was.

Who is the mysterious figure?

An Eerie Tale

They followed Thomas along an alley and into The Prancing Piglet Inn. Jay pulled off her wet boots and soggy socks, and all three sat down in front of the blazing fire.

"I'm so glad you've come back!" Thomas exclaimed. "The amulet must be found. It's all Creville's fault. We're trapped. We can't do anything. So I had to get you back to release us from the curse. I'm sure the amulet's in Gloome Towers . . ."

"Hang on!" Jay said, confused. "What's the amulet? Who's Creville? What's he done?"

"And what's this curse?" Ben gulped, feeling uneasy.

The room fell silent. Outside, the wind began to howl. Ben shivered. Thomas threw another log on the fire, then he leant forward and began to tell them an eerie tale.

Creville dabbled in science and sorcery. At night, luminous mists hung over Creville Manor and sinister wails echoed around its grounds as he carried out his mysterious experiments.

The local lord of the manor was called Sir Gervaise Creville. He owned our village of Wraithe-atte-Mourne.

Creville
always needed
money to buy peculiar things
like unicorns' horns, griffins' tongues
and dragons' teeth for his weird
experiments, so he sold our crops and
animals, leaving us short of food.

Things went from bad to worse and
finally we went to Creville to beg him
to give us food, or we would starve.
We peered through the locked gates
of Creville Manor.

The next day, the Dragon Amulet, our
magic charm, had disappeared from the
ancient statue in the village square. Next
to the statue lay Creville's ring. He had
stolen the amulet to use in experiments
because it has strange powers...

Suddenly there was a flash of purple
light. Seconds later, Creville's dogs
hurled themselves against the gates,
growling ferociously. We fled back to
the village.

The amulet protects the village from
harm. It is made of an unknown gold
metal, shaped like a dragon. No one
knows where it came from, but it has
always been kept in the statue.
According to legend, the village
vanishes if the amulet is taken away...

And from that day the village has been
shrouded in a timeless mist. Although
we're free from Creville, we are trapped
in eternal limbo and have been waiting
for someone to release us.

The Search Begins

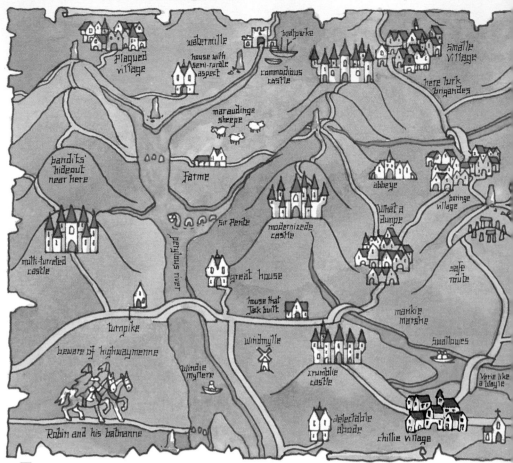

On the map:
plagued village, watermille, boatparke, smalle village, house with semi-rurale aspect, commodious castle, here lurk brigandes, maraudinge sheepe, bandits' hideout near here, Fatme, abbeye, boringe village, Sir Pente, modernizede castle, What a dumpe, multi-turreted castle, great house, safe route, house that Jack built, mankie marshe, turnpike, windmylle, swallowes, beware of highwaymenne, Windie mynere, crumblie castle, Vere like a wayle, Robin and his batmanne, delectable abode, chillie village

J ay and Ben stared at Thomas, aghast. It was a terrible story. But what could they do to help?

"We need you to find the Dragon Amulet and bring it back to the statue," Thomas explained. "Only then will the village be released from limbo."

"But how are we going to find the amulet?" Jay cried. "It could be anywhere!"

"All we know is that Creville stole it," Thomas said. "He probably took it to his secret laboratory in Red Arrow's cell, hidden deep in the dungeons of Gloome Towers.

"But that was over 300 years ago!" exclaimed Ben. "It won't be there now."

"How do you know?" Thomas asked.

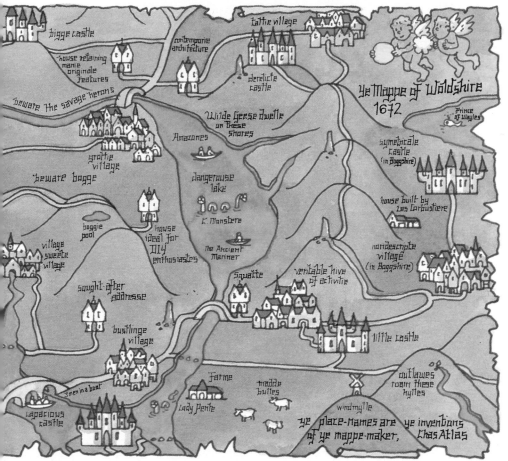

Jay and Ben looked doubtful. It WAS their only lead . . .

"But how do we get back to the village? Tomorrow is the 1st of May," Jay said.

"The village is always here, even if you can't see it," Thomas replied. "When you return to Mourne Valley with the amulet, go to the site of the statue. Then the curse will be lifted."

He unrolled a tattered map and added, "You can see Gloome Towers on here. It's the castle with six turrets."

"That map's ancient," Jay said. "We need to find Gloome Towers on our modern map . . . if it still exists."

Can you find Gloome Towers on Ben's map?
What is the shortest route there?

The Perplexing Plan

Jay clattered along the cobbled lane out of the village. Ben hurried after her. As he ran past the last houses, he felt the same sharp tingle in his neck that he had noticed before.

Gasping for breath, they scrambled up the steep hill to Bleak Moor. When they reached the top, they looked down into Mourne Valley for one last glimpse of the village.

Suddenly, Ben pointed and cried out in amazement. Even as they watched, the valley was growing darker and mistier... the village was vanishing in front of their very eyes!

They raced on across Bleak Moor, leaving Mourne Valley behind, shrouded in darkness. Before long, a ruined castle loomed above them, sinister in the moonlight. This was Gloome Towers, but only one of its six turrets was standing.

Would they still be able to find a way into the dungeons? Jay stared at the heavy turret door. It looked very solid and locked. She grabbed its rusty handle and began to heave and tug. Suddenly the door swung open, sending her flying.

Nervously, Ben peered inside. As his eyes became used to the dark, he could see hundreds of stone steps leading down into the blackness below. On the back of the door hung a tattered piece of parchment. It was a plan of the cells with prisoners' names written on it.

But where was Red Arrow's cell? Ben scanned the plan again and again. Just as he was about to give up hope, a name suddenly caught his eye. Hadn't he seen it in the museum?

Where is Red Arrow's cell? How can they get there?

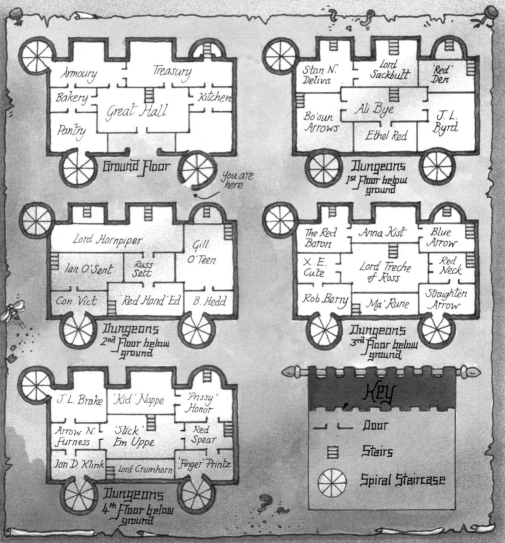

Armoury Treasury

Bakery Great Hall Kitchen

Pantry

Ground Floor

You are here.

Stan N. Deliva Lord Sackbutt 'Red' Den

Bo'sun Arrows Ali Bye J. L. Byrd

Ethel Red

Dungeons 1st Floor below ground

Lord Hornpiper Gill O'Teen

Ian O'Sent Russ Sett

Con Vict 'Red Hand' Ed B. Hedd

Dungeons 2nd Floor below ground

The Red Baron Anna Kist Blue Arrow

X. E. Cute Lord Treche of Ross Red Neck

Rob Berry Ma' Rune Straighten Arrow

Dungeons 3rd Floor below ground

J. L. Brake 'Kid' Nappe 'Prissy' Honor

Arrow N. Furness 'Stick' Em Uppe Red Spear

Ian D. Klink Lord Crumhorn 'Finger' Printz

Dungeons 4th Floor below ground

KEY

— ⌐ Door

▤ Stairs

⊕ Spiral Staircase

Down in the Dungeons

They crept gingerly down the steps to the dungeons. Ben shone his torch into the first cell. It looked empty, so he marched confidently inside. Suddenly the air was filled with beating wings and high-pitched squeals.

"Bats!" he shuddered.

They raced into the next cell and down a flight of steps. They ran on through silent, spooky rooms and stumbled up and down slippery stone stairs until they reached Red Arrow's cell.

Jay shivered. The cell was very creepy. Huge cobwebs hung from the ceiling and everything was covered in a thick layer of dust. Now their search for the amulet began. They peered in pots, crawled under the table and looked in gaps in the wall. But as they had feared, it was nowhere to be found.

A gust of wind whistled through the dingy dungeons. Was that laughter? Jay caught her breath, listening hard. An eerie silence followed. Perhaps she was imagining things.

THUD! The sound came from above. Alarmed, Jay and Ben sprinted back up to the turret door. It had jammed shut. They tugged and heaved as hard as they could, but the door wouldn't budge. They looked at one another in horror.

"Come on," said Ben, trying to sound calm. "Let's try to find another way out."

They raced back down to the dungeons and through a maze of cells. Soon Jay felt completely lost. Perhaps they would never find a way out. They could be trapped for ever in the damp, dark dungeons.

Ben shone his torch ahead but could only see a dead end. There was no way out. He slumped miserably against the wall. With a loud CLICK, a lever sprang shut beneath his right foot. The next second, the wall disappeared and Ben found himself falling backwards. He had discovered another tunnel.

Feeling more hopeful, they followed the passage into a dank room. High above, Ben could see sky. They were at the bottom of a dried-up well.

"We can climb out of here using those ropes and ladders," he said.

Jay was less sure. The ladders had rungs missing and the ropes were old and frayed. But it was their only chance of escape.

Can you find a safe route to the top of the well?

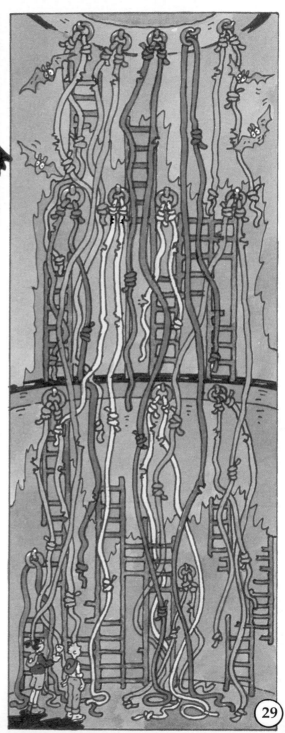

The Deserted House

Jay and Ben clambered out of the well and looked around. They were in the grounds of an old deserted manor house. As Ben gazed up at its sightless windows, he had a strange feeling that someone was watching him. Was that a shadowy figure slipping out of view?

"There's something creepy about this house," he shivered. "Let's get out of here."

"Wait a minute!" hissed Jay.

She stared at a pile of broken statues and crumbling stones in front of the house. The symbols on some of the pieces of stone looked familiar. Then it came to her in a flash. She remembered where she had seen those symbols before and knew where she was.

Where are Jay and Ben?

Cracking Creville's Code

Perhaps the Dragon Amulet was hidden inside Creville Manor. Hundreds of years had passed since Creville lived there. Thomas had said nothing about it being there, but . . .

"We could have a look, just in case," Jay said, as they nervously crept towards the house.

The door creaked open and they stepped inside. When their eyes grew used to the gloom, they realized they were in a large hall.

Jay wandered past the suits of armour, faded tapestries and pewter pots. Then she spotted a book lying on a wooden chest by the window.

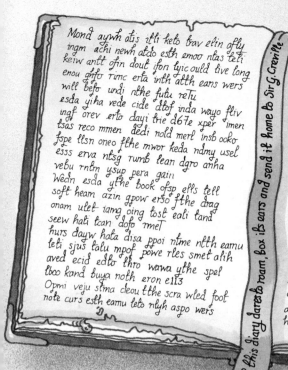

As she blew away the thick layers of dust from its cover, the book fell open at a page covered with spidery writing. But the words made no sense.

"It's Creville's diary," she said, reading the bookmark.

"It might tell us something useful, if we could read it," said Ben, looking over her shoulder.

They stared at the page, baffled. Then Ben realized the writing was in a simple code. Slowly, he began to work out what it said.

BANG! A door slammed somewhere upstairs. An icy draught crept into the hall. Were those footsteps?

Jay and Ben did not stay to find out. They dashed out of the house, across the garden, through the open gates and on into Mourne Valley.

"I know what's happened to the amulet," Ben panted, as he ran. "We've got to go to the stone circle."

What does the diary say?

The King Stone

Soon they were scrambling up the steep hill towards the stone circle. Now they had to find the King Stone and one half of the Dragon Amulet.

Jay stared at the ancient stones. There seemed to be hundreds of them. Some were still upright, while others had toppled over, but there was nothing to show which one was the King Stone.

"This is hopeless," Ben groaned.

"I wonder if the stones have any words or carvings on them," Jay suggested. "Like the . . ."

She stopped, struck by a sudden idea. Of course! The writing on the sundial. They already knew how to find the King Stone.

**The pictures show opposite sides of the big arch in the middle of the stone circle, looking in opposite directions.
Can you spot the King Stone?**

The Missing Piece

As soon as they found the King Stone, they began to dig, using sharp pieces of flint and stone. Seconds later, Ben held an oddly-shaped piece of metal in his hand . . . it was half of the amulet.

Jay stared at the piece of amulet, puzzled. It reminded her of something she had seen before. But what? Then she remembered. The first night, lost on the moor . . . the strange metal object in her soggy boot . . .

"I've already found the other half!" she exclaimed.

She fumbled in her rucksack. It HAD to be there. Frantically, she pulled everything out, then gave the bag a last desperate shake. But the amulet had gone.

What could have happened to it? She racked her brains, but it was no use. There was nothing she could do. The missing piece could be anywhere. Now the vanishing village would remain trapped in limbo for ever.

In gloomy silence, they trudged miserably back to Little Snoozing. As she shuffled along the high street, Jay gazed glumly into the shop windows. Garden gnomes, tartan socks, cuddly toys, huge sticks of Little Snoozing rock and . . .

The missing half of the amulet! She stared open-mouthed in disbelief.

**Where is the missing piece of the amulet?
How did it get there?**

Returning the Amulet

The shopkeeper remembered them from the cafe and gave the piece of amulet back to Jay.

"I thought it was just an old brooch," he smiled. "Ideal for my window display."

"There's no time to lose!" Ben exclaimed, speeding out of the shop. "We've got to get back to Mourne Valley."

When they reached the valley, they found a wood where the village should have been.

"But Wraithe IS still here," said Jay, ducking under a low branch. "We just can't see it."

It was strange to think that they were walking down invisible streets past houses and people. Somewhere among the trees was the site of the statue.

Suddenly Ben heard the sound of rushing water. He pushed through some bushes into a small clearing.

"I'm sure this is the river which ran through the village square," he said. "We must be near the right place now."

The trees by the river looked very old. Ben thought he had seen some of them before.

This gave him an idea. He began drawing imaginary lines between trees and boulders.

"I know where the statue is," he yelled. "Follow me!"

Where should the statue be?

Clutching the two halves of the Dragon Amulet, they rushed to the spot where the lines met . . . A sharp tingle ran down their necks. The ground shook beneath their feet. In the distance, a bell began to toll. Each stroke sounded nearer and nearer. A clock struck twelve . . .

Jay and Ben blinked, then stared, dazed. They were in a bustling village square. A boy waved as he walked towards them. He looked very familiar.

"What's happened?" Ben gasped. "Who are you?"

"Tom, you idiot," the boy said, puzzled. "Don't you remember?"

"Where are we?" Ben asked.

"In Wraith-at-Mourne, of course," Tom laughed.

"But that's impossible!" Ben exclaimed.

"Why?" said a voice.

Ben turned and saw Aunt Hetty sitting at her easel, smiling at them. As he glanced at the shops around the square, he gaped in disbelief. Wraith was a modern village! It was as if the village had never vanished. But that was impossible – or was it? Could they have changed the course of history when they returned with the amulet?

But where was the amulet? It had disappeared! Had someone stolen it? Would the village vanish again? Jay wandered around for a while, feeling anxious.

Then she smiled. She knew the amulet was safe.

Where is the amulet?

The Three Strangers

Later that day, Tom climbed the steep path to Bleak Moor with Jay and Ben trailing behind. They were off to explore the ruined castle on Wildmoor Hill, which was haunted by a headless woman in green.

"You two are acting very strangely," Tom said. "What's the matter?"

Jay tried to explain about the vanishing village, the amulet and the curse, but Tom just thought it was a good story.

As they reached the top of the moor, Ben spotted three people a little way ahead. He nudged Jay. Hadn't they seen them before?

As the figures came closer, Jay and Ben saw their faces clearly for the first time. They gasped...

Then Jay chuckled. She knew who the three strangers were. And she guessed they weren't too pleased. Nothing had worked out quite as they planned.

Who are the three strangers?

Clues

Pages 4-5

This is a trick question. Look on the map for the landmarks in the picture. Don't worry if you can't find the village.

Pages 6-7

This is easy. Use your eyes.

Pages 10-11

Combine the two messages, taking one word from one message and one word from the other, then two words from one and two from the other. Repeat this pattern until you run out of words.

Pages 12-13

Look at the posters. How do they match up with what people are saying?

Pages 14-15

Look carefully at the lists of villages in Woldshire. Most villages appear on all lists, but three do not. What are their names? Look at Ben's map on page 5.

Pages 16-17

Match the carvings on the stone with the symbols in the book.

Pages 18-19

Can you see anything from the inn?

Pages 20-21

He has appeared before.

Pages 24-25

Compare Thomas's map with Ben's map. Can you match up the positions of the rivers and the lake? Gloome Towers could now be a ruin.

Pages 26-27

Does Red Arrow have another name? This is a three-dimensional maze.

Pages 28-29

This is easy, but make sure the ropes are knotted at the top.

Pages 30-31

Some of the pieces have similar markings. Try joining them together. Do you recognize them?

Pages 32-33

The gaps between the words are not in the right places.

Pages 34-35

Look at the description of the standing stones and the carved message on the sundial on page 17. Remember the sun rises in the east.

Pages 36-37

What does the other half of the amulet look like? Turn to page 4 if you can't remember. Then use your eyes.

Pages 38-39

Look at the village square on page 21. Do you recognize any trees or boulders?

Pages 40-41

This is easy if you know what's on in Wraith.

Page 42

Flick back through the book and look at Creville's diary on page 33.

Answers

Pages 4-5

Jay and Ben are standing beside Bleak Pool. This is the only pool on the map so it must be the one Jay fell into. This means they are on Bleak Moor. The picture on page 5 shows the view looking north-east. Through the mist they can see the standing stones on top of Sombre Hill, the ruin on Gale Edge and the small river that runs into River Mourne. The village is in Mourne Valley but it is not marked on the map. The mystery begins...

Jay and Ben are here   The village is here

Pages 6-7

This is The Prancing Piglet Inn. ———

Pages 10-11

The words from both messages must be fitted together to work out what the complete message says. Take one word from Jay's message, then one from Ben's, followed by two words from Jay's and two from Ben's. Follow this pattern of one word followed by two words from each message (always taking the words in the order they appear), until you run out of words.

This is what the complete message says:

We need your help. The ancient curse has taken its terrible revenge. Our village has vanished and we are trapped in eternal limbo. Only you can release us. Please come back to us and I will explain everything. But remember that you must bring something from the village with you.

Pages 12-13

The old man with the white beard says there is an old tale of a mysterious village in Mourne Valley. This was the site of the village that Jay and Ben visited last night. Ben has seen the poster advertizing a jumble sale on the 30th of April. When he hears the man in the checked waistcoat say he is going to the jumble sale, Ben realizes the 30th of April is today.

According to the man with the newspaper, the ghostly village appears only on "the last three days of the fourth month", in other words, the 28th, 29th and 30th of April. Jay and Ben saw the village in Mourne Valley last night, the 29th of April. Perhaps the old tales could be true. If so, the village should appear again tonight for the last time this year.

Pages 14-15

Jay discovers the name of the village in Mourne Valley by looking at the lists. The name of every village on these lists appears on Ben's map, except Wraithe-atte-Mourne.

Wraithe-atte-Mourne appears for the last time on the list dated March 1672. It is not marked on the list dated May 1672. Since the lists cover ALL the villages in Woldshire, this must mean that Wraithe-atte-Mourne no longer exists in May 1672.

The lists do not say where Wraithe-atte-Mourne was, but Jay remembers a picture on the wall of the inn on page 9 showing "The Village in Mourne Valley", dated March 1672. From this, she deduces that Wraithe-atte-Mourne, the village that vanished from the lists, is the village in Mourne Valley.

It looks as though Wraithe-atte-Mourne is the village that appeared in Mourne Valley last night.

Pages 16-17

The symbols on the sundial stand for letters, numbers and full stops, but there are no gaps between words. This is what the inscription on the sundial says with punctuation and word spaces added:

Bare Wilf stood on the hillside and looked eastwards. He walked to the lone sentry stone on the south-west edge of the stones. Then he walked in a straight line due east, passing a row of 7 stones, 2 rows of 4 stones, a row of 5 stones and the lone ranger stone. Then he reached another row of 5 stones. He climbed over the southernmost stone, then passed a row of 3 stones. Next, he walked northwards for a short way up to the queen stone that stands in a row by itself. Turning east again, he stood right in front of the king stone. He sprinkled it with the magic water. Instantly the spell was broken. The king thanked Bare Wilf and gave him all his mugs.

Pages 18-19

Ben has spotted a silver spoon which he recognizes from The Prancing Piglet Inn.

Here it is.

Pages 20-21

The figure is Thomas, the boy they met in the inn on pages 8 and 9.

Pages 24-25

On the map there is a note saying that the names of places are not real but are inventions of the map maker. The only castle with six turrets is "crumblie castle". This must be Gloome Towers.

You can match up Thomas's and Ben's maps by comparing the positions of the lake, rivers, villages and other landmarks, although finding out where hills are is trickier, as the two maps show hills in different ways. By doing this, you can locate the position of Gloome Towers as the ruin on Wetterstill Hill.

When Jay and Ben leave the village, they will return to the present and must use Ben's map to find their way to Gloome Towers. The route is marked in black.

Gloome Towers

Pages 26-27

Red Arrow is Lord Crumhorn (see page 15). To reach his cell, they first go down the turret stairs to the second floor of the dungeons and then they go through the cells as numbered here:

Start here →

Lord Crumhorn's cell →

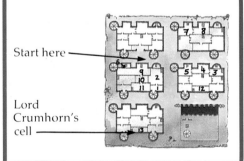

Pages 28-29

The safe route is marked in black.

Pages 30-31

Jay has spotted broken pieces of Sir Gervaise Creville's crest, which she saw in the museum on page 15. The crest has crumbled away from the wall above the door. They are in the grounds of Creville Manor, Creville's home.

Here is the crest when it is pieced together.

Pages 32-33

The gaps between the words in the diary have been removed and the letters have been divided into groups of four. This is what the diary says with the gaps between the words put in the right places and punctuation added:

Monday: What is it like to travel in a flying machine? What does the moon taste like? I want to find out. If only I could live long enough – for I'm certain that the answers will be found in the future.

Tuesday: I have decided to find a way of living for ever. Today I tried 67 experiments, as recommended in Old Merlin's Book of Spells. None of them worked. And my useless servants, Grumble and Groan, have burnt my supper again.

Wednesday: The Book of Spells tells of the amazing powers of the Dragon Amulet. I am going to steal it and see what it can do for me.

Thursday: What a disappointment. The amulet is just a lump of powerless metal. I have decided to throw away the spell book and buy another one.

11.30 pm: I've just made out the scrawled footnote. Curses! The amulet only has powers to help that wretched village. If I can't use the amulet, no one else is going to use it.

Friday: Tee hee! What a shock those villagers will have when they see that their precious amulet has gone. And they'll never find it – I've broken the amulet in two and hidden one piece under the King Stone in the stone circle. I hurled the other at some sheep on the moors. May the villagers all live miserably ever after.

Saturday: I've found a way to live for ever. Only one vital ingredient was missing.

Curses! It's worked, but I may have done something slightly wrong. I'm here for ever, but stuck in my horrid brown cloak, and, even worse, I seem to have brought Groan and Grumble with me. Now they never leave my side. How I hate the sight of them already! Aaaargh!

Pages 34-35

The inscription on the sundial on page 17 tells them how to find the King Stone.

Their route to the King Stone is marked in red.

The book on page 17 says that the stones are arranged in rows running north to south. Each stone in the first row mentioned in the inscription (a row of seven stones) is marked with an asterisk.

The Lone Ranger Stone

The rising sun in the east

The Queen Stone

The King Stone

The route goes behind this stone.

The Sentry Stone

Two stones make up this arch.

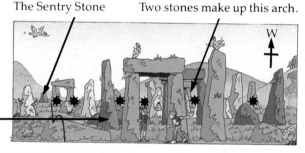

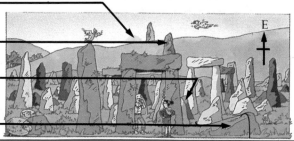

Pages 36-37

Here is the missing piece of the amulet.

The shopkeeper picked it up in the cafe on page 13, where it fell out of Jay's rucksack.

Pages 38-39

Ben remembers that the statue stood in the centre of the village square (see page 21). He recognizes six landmarks that bordered the square. He can locate the statue's position by drawing lines between the six landmarks as shown:

Chestnut tree

Stone

Stepping stone

The statue should be here

Tree stump

Holly bush

Oak tree

Pages 40-41

The poster on the notice board shows that the Dragon Amulet is in Wraith Museum.

Page 42

The three strangers are Sir Gervaise Creville and his servants, Grumble and Groan. Jay and Ben recognize Creville from his portrait on page 8, and Grumble and Groan from their identity cards in the museum on page 15.

Remembering Creville's diary on page 33, Jay knows that Creville cast a spell to make him live for ever but his plans went slightly wrong. He has to wear his horrid cloak and his hated servants, Grumble and Groan, will never leave his side. This may explain his grumpy expression.

First published in 1990 by
Usborne Publishing Ltd,
Usborne House,
83-85 Saffron Hill,
London EC1N 8RT, England

Copyright © 1990 Usborne Publishing Ltd.

The name Usborne and the device 🐣 are Trade Marks of Usborne Publishing Ltd.

Printed in Italy.